FIRST SNOW

Nancy Viau
pictures by Talitha Shipman

Albert Whitman & Company
Chicago, Illinois

To the mitten finders, snow shovelers, igloo architects,
and sled drivers—all the grown-ups who help children experience
the wonder of a snowy day—NV

To Coral, the Abominable Snow Baby—TS

Library of Congress Cataloging-in-Publication Data

Names: Viau, Nancy, author. | Shipman, Talitha, illustrator.
Title: First snow / Nancy Viau; pictures by Talitha Shipman.
Description: Chicago, Illinois: Albert Whitman & Company, 2018. |
Summary: Neighbors don their winter gear and head into the icy air to build snowmen
and igloos, race sleds, and throw snowballs before returning to the warmth of their homes.
Identifiers: LCCN 2017061613 | ISBN 978-0-8075-2440-4 (hardcover)
Subjects: | CYAC: Stories in rhyme. | Snow—Fiction. | Play—Fiction. | Neighbors—Fiction.
Classification: LCC PZ8.3.V712667 Fir 2018 | DDC [E]—dc23
LC record available at https://lccn.loc.gov/2017061613

Pictures by Talitha Shipman
First published in the United States of America in 2018 by Albert Whitman & Company

Printed in China
10 9 8 7 6 5 4 3 2 1 HH 22 21 20 19 18

Design by Rick DeMonico

For more information about Albert Whitman & Company,
visit our website at www.albertwhitman.com.

Perky faces.
Scrambling feet.

Snowflakes falling!
What a treat!

Puffy jackets. Scarves in place.

Extra mittens, just in case.

Clunky boots and funky hats.

Hurry! Scurry!
Don’t look back!

Frisky puppy leads the way.
Join the neighbors.
Shout, "Hooray!"

Rosy cheeks. An icy air.
Catch a flake, without a care.

Silly snowman. Crooked nose.

With his hat, he strikes a pose.

Cozy igloo. Wintry bed.

Time’s a-wasting. Get the sled!

Noisy voices. Toothy grins.
Fearless racers. Guess who wins!

Weary bodies.
Not quite beat.

Snowball fight across the street.

Friendly ending. Wave of hands.

Snow fun done in wonderland.

Creamy chocolate—warm, not cold.

Peaceful twilight. Stories told.

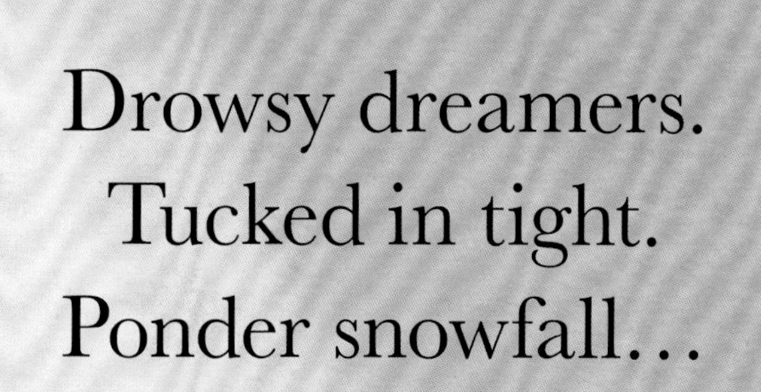

Drowsy dreamers.
Tucked in tight.
Ponder snowfall…

overnight.